Saving Squeak:
The Otter Tale

Jennifer Keats Curtis

Illustrated by
Marcy Dunn Ramsey

"Otter"ly enjoy!
♡, *[signature]*

Schiffer Publishing Ltd

4880 Lower Valley Road · Atglen, Pennsylvania 19310

Other Schiffer Books By The Author:
Osprey Adventure, 978-0-87033-593-8, $13.95

Other Schiffer Books on Related Subjects:
Mother Monarch, 978-0-7643-3400-9, $19.99
Beddy Bye in the Bay, 978-0-7643-3450-4, $14.99
Chadwick the Crab, 978-0-87033-347-7

Schiffer Books are available at special discounts for bulk purchases for sales promotions or premiums. Special editions, including personalized covers, corporate imprints, and excerpts can be created in large quantities for special needs. For more information contact the publisher:

Published by Schiffer Publishing Ltd.
4880 Lower Valley Road
Atglen, PA 19310
Phone: (610) 593-1777; Fax: (610) 593-2002
E-mail: Info@schifferbooks.com

For the largest selection of fine reference books on this and related subjects,

please visit our web site at **www.schifferbooks.com**
We are always looking for people to write books on new and related subjects.
If you have an idea for a book please contact us at the above address.

This book may be purchased from the publisher.
Include $5.00 for shipping.
Please try your bookstore first.

You may write for a free catalog.

In Europe, Schiffer books are distributed by
Bushwood Books
6 Marksbury Ave.
Kew Gardens
Surrey TW9 4JF England
Phone: 44 (0) 20 8392 8585; Fax: 44 (0) 20 8392 9876
E-mail: info@bushwoodbooks.co.uk
Website: www.bushwoodbooks.co.uk

To the world's best in-laws,
Maureen Curtis & John Jett,
and the real Braden.

Thinking about that last goal in his lacrosse game, Braden nearly missed the curled-up, brown fur ball under the sagging park bench.

As Braden approached, the dark-pelted animal lifted his grayish face and uttered a mewing sound.

A kitten?

Braden squatted down for a better look.

The baby's fur was soft and fluffy, like a young cat's, but underneath, a soft black nose and long, white whiskers protruded.

A puppy?

The baby extended one paw—a webbed paw with long claws.

Baby otter!

What was a baby otter doing at the park?

Braden wasn't sure, but he knew better than to touch a wild animal, even a young one. He phoned for help.

Within minutes, Braden's parents arrived. Gently, Braden's mother wrapped the otter in a towel and placed him in a small box. Silently, the otter peered at them with small, brown eyes.

Although Braden didn't have much experience with wild animals, he could see that this one was tired and weak. His mother said she had already called a wildlife rehabilitator for help. A rehabilitator is an expert who cares for injured or orphaned wild animals and then returns them to nature when possible.

On the car ride to the rehabilitator's, Braden dreamed of keeping the otter as a pet. Wouldn't his friends be jealous when he and the otter sledded down the big hill behind their house together? Could he keep the otter in the bathtub? What would he name him? Or was it a girl?

Braden's dream was rudely interrupted as a woman dressed in blue scrubs rushed out to meet them. She quickly took the otter back to the center, thanking Braden and his parents for their help.

Back in the car, Braden's mother told him that although river otters appear cute and sweet, they are wild animals, not to be tamed as pets. Otters can be quick-tempered and have the bite to prove it.

The next day, Suzanne, the rehabilitator, called Braden with an update:

"Otters are extremely good mothers and rarely leave their young pups alone. Since you saw this little otter on his own, he probably was lost, which can happen on the first trip out of the den.

Your otter is about three months old. I'll need to bottle feed him about six times a day to help him gain weight and get healthy. Hopefully, we will be able to release him near the river where you found him.

I know you want to help, but we work with wild animals, so children are not permitted in the rehabilitation center."

Braden was disappointed, but he understood. Besides, he had already played an important role by finding the right person to care for the otter. He was partly responsible for the otter getting well.

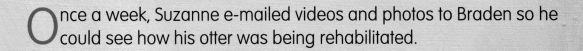

Once a week, Suzanne e-mailed videos and photos to Braden so he could see how his otter was being rehabilitated.

At first, when Suzanne tried to feed the baby, the otter screamed and bit at the nipple on the bottle. In time, he learned to nurse readily. By the end of the second week, the otter had figured out that Suzanne was the "food lady." Braden asked Suzanne if they could name the otter Squeak, the noise the little mammal made while nursing.

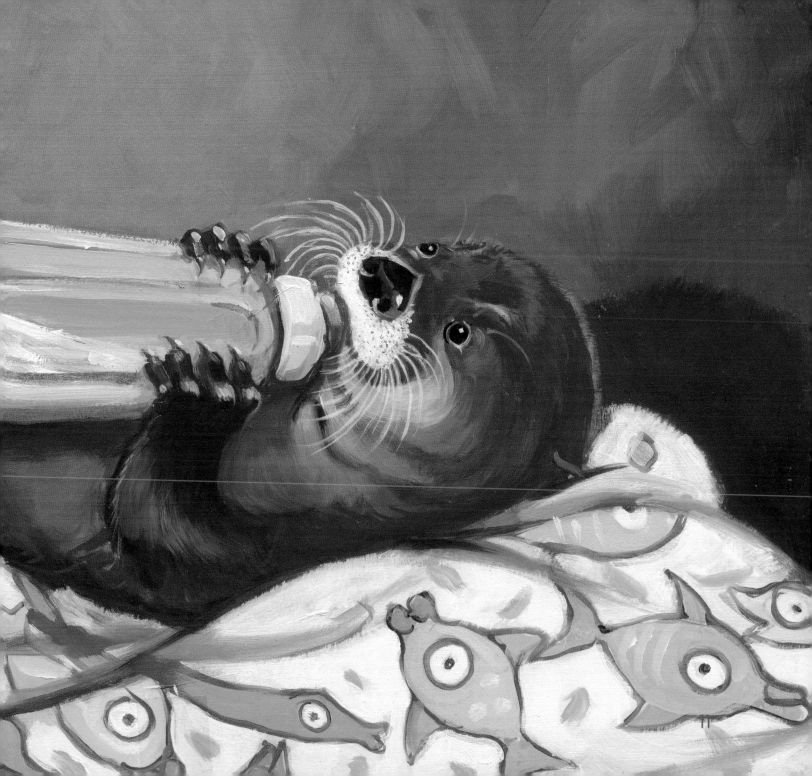

Through phone calls and e-mails, Braden got a chance to know the otter. His favorite photo was of Suzanne using otter puppets to play with Squeak. Although nipping is part of otter play, even little nips can leave big bruises on humans, explained Suzanne.

At four months, Squeak's swimming lessons began. Otters' sleek bodies, webbed paws, and powerful tails are made for swimming. They can, in fact, swim faster than most fish. But, first, they must learn how. In the wild, otter mothers carry their pups into the water and teach them to swim. Once Squeak learned to master blowing bubbles in a small dog bowl, Suzanne encouraged him to put his face in a baby tub of water, and then slip and slide in a half-filled kiddie pool. At six months, Squeak was swimming, really swimming, just like an otter, in the center's large pool.

At seven months—the same age as wild river otters—Squeak learned to fish. After eating small bites of cut-up fish, the 11-pound pup seemed eager to hunt on his own. Suzanne placed fish in a shallow tub and allowed him to catch them before putting the "prey" into the big pool and allowing him to swim after them.

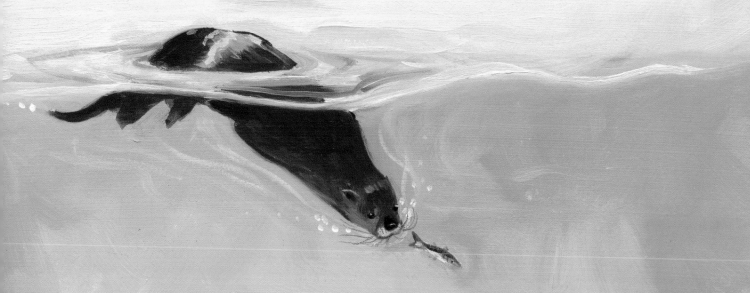

At nine months—when Squeak's mom would have encouraged him to go on his own—Suzanne called Braden. Squeak can't be released, she sighed. He won't be able to feed himself because his teeth are just not healthy enough to chew whole fish.

Braden was upset. What would this mean for Squeak? Suzanne said they needed to find him a permanent home, but not at Braden's house!

Braden researched river otters online. He and Suzanne called other wildlife rehabilitation centers to ask questions. Together they learned that a nearby museum wanted an otter for their exhibit.

A few days later, an aquarist, an expert who cares for animals that live in tanks, took Squeak to the museum. He would be joining another rescued otter who was about the same age.

Braden couldn't wait to visit Squeak and his new "brother," Bubbles!

During his first visit to Squeak's new home, Braden peeked through the door of the otter holding area in the back of the museum. Most visitors are not allowed here, but as Squeak's rescuer, Braden has special privileges.

Braden saw a diamond-shaped black nose and long, white whiskers peeking over the top of a big, polka-dotted towel. Wrapped like a baby in a blanket, Bubbles lounged lazily in a green hammock.

Without warning, Squeak grabbed the towel with his teeth and yanked. Hard.

The sleepy otter fell out of the hammock with a thump and tried to wriggle free of his wrap.

Still holding the towel in his sharp teeth, Squeak crept backward, pulling the towel with all of his might. Like a Slinky®, Squeak's body coiled and unfolded, coiled and unfolded. Using his strong thick tail, he inched toward the door. Finally, he yanked the towel free from Bubbles' body.

Bubbles shrieked. Squeak chirped. Braden laughed.

With Squeak in the lead, the furry otters banged through a small flap that led to the cool tank of water outside.

Braden dashed out to follow the otters to the huge habitat. In awe, he watched the sleek mammals flip and twirl. They swam upside down and on their backs, mermaid-like, cheerfully bobbing along the water near the glass window, as if to say, "Hello," to him. When Braden dashed alongside the glass, Squeak followed him.

In winter, with their double coats keeping them warm and waterproofed, the otters like nothing better than to swim after snowballs. Braden heaved one into the tank. The otters pushed through the water with their powerful tails, chasing it, then came back to the glass to see if Braden was watching. Show-offs!

Linda, the aquarist, grinned and tossed a dog biscuit into the water for each of them (since no one makes otter treats).

In the wild, otters are more nocturnal. They burrow during the day and fish at night. However, Squeak and Bubbles have cheerfully adapted to the museum's daytime routine.

In nature, otters are great at finding prey in the water. They use their long whiskers to feel vibrations created when other animals, like fish or frogs, move in the water. In murky water, otters use their paws like fingers to feel for fish, snakes, and even snails. In shallow water, otters might slap their tails to scare these animals into a cove where they can be easily trapped and eaten.

Bubbles and Squeak are lucky. Rather than spending time hunting for food, handlers bring them inside each day and feed them cut-up fish, oily capelin, and stinky smelt. Yum! The otters gently take turns grabbing the fish from the handler and gulping it down like seals. However, river otters are not in the seal family. They are members of the Mustelidae family, which includes ferrets, weasels, skunks, and badgers. And, they have the musky scent to prove it!

When feeding time is over, the handler gives each otter one cut-up carrot to signal that meal time is over. It is time to go back outside to play.

Like wild otters, Bubbles and Squeak spend their time eating, sleeping, and playing. Their handlers have learned how important it is to keep them entertained and busy. Otherwise, they fight, much like brothers. Since there are no "otter toys," the handlers offer baby toys, Frisbees, and homemade playthings, like tough containers and durable pipes. Bubbles' favorite is a plastic jar with a screw-off lid. He stomps on it, throws it, kicks it, and pushes it with his nose before opening it with his paws to see what, if anything, is inside. Squeak, of course, likes nothing better than to wait for his brother to wrap himself in a towel and fall asleep so he can yank it off and let the game of chase begin again.

In the wild, busy beavers build dens and hard-working muskrats build lodges. Crafty otters don't bother to build nests. They take over abandoned burrows or find cavities created by the roots of a tree that has fallen over alongside the shore.

In captivity, the otters are even lazier. After they exhaust themselves playing, they often wriggle around in the sand to dry off, then nap together outside in a hollowed-out log or inside on their hammocks.

Braden smiled. As the brothers curled up peacefully, he snapped a photo. He still wished he and Squeak could sled together, but he was glad that his otter is safe and happy.

Once common throughout America's waterways, river otters were nearly hunted to extinction for their thick, soft fur. Today, thanks to efforts to save them, otters are making a comeback. Due to development and pollution, otters sometimes are found among humans. Should you find an otter in trouble, do not try to rescue him yourself. To find the wildlife rehabilitator nearest you, visit http://wildliferehabinfo.org

This book is based on the work of wildlife rehabilitator Suzanne McBride, who helps return healthy river otters and other creatures to the wild. Bubbles and Squeak are real otters who were abandoned as pups and rescued. They now reside at the Calvert Marine Museum in Solomons Island, Maryland. They are cared for by doting aquarists, like Linda Hanna, who enjoy the antics and games of the furry mammals.

It is expensive to rehabilitate and care for otters; therefore, a portion of the royalties from this book is donated to Wildlife Response, Inc. (www.wildliferesponse.org). Another portion is donated to the Calvert Marine Museum so that Squeak and Bubbles will be around to show off for visitors for years to come.

–Jennifer Keats Curtis